Series 497

NED
THE LONELY DONKEY

A Story by
NOEL BARR

Illustrations by
P. B. HICKLING

Publishers: Wills & Hepworth Ltd., Loughborough
PRINTED IN ENGLAND

NED, THE LONELY DONKEY

Ned, the little grey donkey, had lived all alone on his hill for as long as he could remember. He had lived there, among the furze bushes and near the little hurrying stream in summer and in winter, in sunshine and in rain.

One sunny afternoon after he had run races with his shadow and jumped the stream over and over again, he felt tired and thirsty. He took a long drink of cool water, and lay down on the short springy grass.

He got up and went to look for a sheep. There were very few of them on the hill, and they were generally too busy eating to have any time for talking. At last he found one.

"Are you lonely?" he asked.

"Lonely?" said the sheep, lifting her head from the grass, "lonely? I never have time to think about it; are you?"

"Yes, I think I am," said Ned. "I'd like someone to talk to and play with."

"I've no time for things like that," said the sheep. "Eating grass takes all my time," and she went on eating grass as if she could never get enough.

Ned walked slowly away. "I don't want to eat all the time," he thought. "I like doing other things ; eating isn't everything." Just then he met a hurrying rabbit.

"Wait a minute," he called. The rabbit stopped and turned round.

"Yes," she said, "what is it ? I've no time to spare."

"Are you lonely ?" asked Ned.

"Lonely ?" cried the rabbit. "Me lonely ? I've a husband and eight children, and you can't be lonely with a family like that ! I must go, the children will be getting into mischief and my husband will soon be home," and away she went.

Ned started to go back to the stream and the thick furze bush that kept the wind off him at night. He stopped suddenly, for he had almost stepped on a peewit sitting on her nest.

" Oh dear—" he began, " I hope—"

" No, you didn't hurt me," said the peewit, " but you really should look where you're going, you know."

" Yes," agreed Ned. " I'm afraid I was thinking."

" What about ? " asked the peewit.

" I've decided that I'm lonely," the little donkey said, " and I'm wondering what I can do about it."

The peewit put her head on one side and looked at him with her bright eyes. " Go and ask the wise owl in the dark wood," she said.

That evening Ned trotted by the light of the moon to look for the wise owl. There were queer noises in the wood, and frightening shadows made him jump, but he went on until he was in the thickest part of it. Then he stopped and listened.

"Whoo-hoo-hoo-oo," he heard, "whoo-hoo-oo!" Ned went slowly and carefully through the trees and tangled bushes, and at last he saw the wise owl sitting on a branch of a large oak tree. He was brown, with large round eyes, and he really did look very wise.

The owl looked down at Ned and asked him what he wanted.

"I've come to ask for your help," Ned said. "I live up on the hill, among the furze bushes and near a little stream. Sometimes I see a sheep, and sometimes a rabbit, but they have no time to spare. I play by myself, I eat by myself, and I sleep by myself; and I am lonely. What can I do about it?"

The owl stared at him, then he shut his eyes for a moment.

"The best thing to do," he said, "is to find someone else who is lonely, because if you put two lonely people together, usually neither of them is lonely any more."

"I see," said Ned, as he nodded his head. "Thank you very much indeed." And he trotted away.

Next morning the grey donkey galloped down the hill to the farm in the valley. He looked in all the fields for a little donkey like himself, but there wasn't one to be seen. He talked to some black and white cows.

" I thought there might be a lonely donkey here like me," he said.

" I don't think you will find anyone lonely here," answered one of the cows. " We aren't, there are so many of us," and they all moved away to a very green stretch of grass.

Ned spoke to some pigs in the sty, but they only opened their sleepy eyes for a moment before shutting them again.

There were two big brown horses harnessed to a plough in one of the fields. Ned asked them whether he would be able to stay at the farm, but they thought not.

"You see," they told him, "everyone here has something to do, and that may be why they never have time to think of being lonely. But a donkey, well, what can a donkey do?"

"Nothing special, I suppose," Ned said sadly. "No, I can't think of anything I could do really well. I can quite understand that I would still be lonely here." And he trotted away down the high road.

Very soon he overtook an old man with a sack over his shoulder.

"Hullo, little fellow," said the old man, "you are just what I'm looking for," and he put a rope round Ned's neck and led him towards his cottage.

"I do believe I've found someone just as lonely as I am," thought Ned, and he felt very happy.

The old man tied Ned to the gate post and opened the door. His wife came to meet him and so did his dog, and a white cat leapt on to his shoulder.

"Look what I've found," the old man said to his wife. "Think how useful he'll be, my sacks can go in a little cart now."

So Ned was put into a little shed where he had very little room. The old man was glad to have him but quite forgot to give him anything to eat.

"He can't be lonely," thought Ned. "He has his wife and his cat and his dog; and I don't like being here."

He kicked hard on the shed door, and when the old man came to see what he wanted he pushed past him and galloped away down the road.

After a little time he reached the edge of a cliff and looked down at the sea.

"What a lot of water," he thought, "and how blue it is." Then he saw the yellow sand, and the children playing and paddling.

"It looks very pleasant," said Ned out loud; and a sea-gull, overhearing him, said: "It is, you know."

Ned was going to answer him when he suddenly forgot all about the sea and the sand and the sea-gull, for he had seen a little group of donkeys just below him.

"My goodness, those are donkeys like me!" he said. "Perhaps they'll let me stay with them, and then I'll never be lonely again," and he found a crooked little path and made his way down to the shore.

But the donkeys laughed at him because he came from the country and knew nothing about a sea-side donkey's life. They told him he could give the next ride and see how he liked it; so a very fat, almost-grown-up boy climbed on to his back and he started off. How heavy the boy was, and how hot and uncomfortable the sand was; so different from the cool grass on his hill. The other donkeys laughed again when he got back, tired and out of breath. They told him he would never make a sea-side donkey, and they turned their backs on him and talked among themselves.

Ned turned away and went sadly up the cliff.

"I don't seem to be able to find anyone as lonely as I am," he thought. "I'll go and ask the wise owl to think of something else." So he trotted all the way back to the dark wood and listened for the wise owl.

"Whoo-hoo-oo," he heard, and this time he found the owl sitting in a beech tree.

They talked for a long time, but the owl couldn't think of anything else and Ned went slowly back to his hill to live as before.

On the following morning he ran races with his shadow and jumped the stream two or three times, and then had a long drink. As he was resting on the cool grass a magpie flew down and sat on a large stone nearby.

"I heard what you were saying to the wise owl last night," it said.

"Did you?" replied Ned, "I didn't see you."

"It was dark in the wood," the magpie said. "I've been thinking about you. Will you come with me? I want to show you something."

Ned got up and he and the magpie went down the hill and through the fields together. Ned trotted briskly and the magpie flew beside him. After a time they came to a road, and in the road were some large iron gates.

"You must go through these," the magpie said.

"Through these?" But where are you taking me?" Ned asked, feeling very puzzled.

"You'll soon see," was all the magpie said in reply, and they went up a long drive with flowering bushes on either side, and green lawns beyond. And then, as they went round a bend, they met a man wheeling a wheel-barrow.

"Hey you!" he called out, taking hold of Ned by his mane, "turn round and go out again, little donkey, you don't live here, you know," and he led Ned all the way back to the big gates.

"I don't like putting you out in the road, old chap," he said, "but I expect you'll soon find your way home," and he led the little donkey through and closed the gates behind him.

The magpie, who had flown up into a tree when the gardener had appeared, now came down again.

"Never mind," it said, "I know another way in."

He took Ned along the road for a little way, and then told him to push his way through a gap in the hedge. When Ned had done this they went through the bushes until the magpie said they were to stop.

"Look," it said, "over there, can you see him?"

Ned looked across a stretch of green lawn and saw the gardener busily sweeping the path. "That man?" he said, "yes, I see him, he'll send us away again if he sees us."

"No no," said the magpie, "not the gardener; look there, in the middle of the lawn."

Ned looked again and saw a little boy sitting on a garden chair. He was all alone and he sat quite still, staring in front of him. There were a few toys on the grass but he had none in his hands.

"He looks—he looks lonely," Ned said to the magpie.

"He is lonely," the magpie said. "His mother and father have been away for some time and he has nobody to play with. Oh, he's looked after well enough, but he's lonely, and that's why I brought you."

"Oh," said Ned. "I see—yes, of course I see, and the next moment he was trotting across the lawn. The little boy, whose name was Timothy, jumped up and stared, then he ran forward, put his arms round Ned's neck and hugged him.

"Oh," he cried, "have you come to play with me? Have you come to live with me? May I have a ride on your back?"

He climbed on to Ned's back and held firmly to his mane, and Ned trotted round the lawn, with the magpie watching from a tree close by. Then the gardener saw them, threw down his broom and hurried towards them.

"Hey, what's happening here?" he cried, taking hold of Timothy's arm as if he might fall off Ned's back. "Whose donkey is this? I've just put him outside the gates."

"He's going to be mine!" said Timothy excitedly, "come along and let's make a stable for him."

"But—but someone will claim him, he isn't really yours, you know," the gardener said, looking worried, and rubbing his chin.

"I'll keep him until someone does," said Timothy, "but oh, I hope no one will, I want him for my very own. Come and see about the stable, will you?"

"Well, well, I suppose I must," the gardener said, shaking his head, but smiling at the same time.

The little donkey was taken to a comfortable shed at the other end of the garden, and the magpie flew away calling out that he would soon see Ned again. Timothy and the gardener worked very hard, they put hay and water ready for Ned, and clean straw on the floor. After Ned had had a rest, Timothy climbed on to his back, and they went slowly round and round the large garden.

Something was happening to Ned, and slowly he understood what it was.

" The wise owl was right," he said to himself, " I'm not lonely any more, and I don't think Timothy is either. And the horses were right, too, about doing things."

The old aunt who was looking after Timothy made rather a fuss and was sure that Ned belonged to someone, but at last she said she would try to find out and that he could stay until she had done so.

Ned thought it was very funny.

"As if I ever belonged to anyone," he said to himself. " I have always been alone."

But now he wasn't alone any more, for he and Timothy were always together and Ned grew fatter and Timothy grew rosier. And then Timothy had another surprise.

One day he was running races with Ned when a car drove slowly up the drive and then stopped. Timothy could hardly believe his eyes when he saw his mother and father get out of it. He and Ned ran as fast as they could, and the next moment there was a muddle of three people and a small grey donkey all hugging one another. After Timothy had explained all about Ned, his father said that if no one claimed the little donkey, Timothy could certainly keep him.

So Ned lived with Timothy, and one day he went to the edge of the dark wood with the boy on his back. The wise owl saw him coming and flew to a tree close by

"Not lonely any more, are you?" he asked.

"No, thank you," answered Ned, "not any more, and neither is Timothy. Thank you very much for helping me."

Very often, when the nights were long and Timothy was in bed, Ned would lie on the grass talking to the magpie in the tree above him. The magpie would tell Ned about the hill with the furze bushes and the hurrying stream, and Ned would tell him all about Timothy.